The Cynic's View of

Laborious

Chores

Kevin H. Hilton

Doing the dishes without a dishwasher could so easily become a four times a day chore, unless of course everything is left to mount up in the sink.

Hattie Quicksilver has come upon another solution. Adding anxiety to the task, she turns her special bowl to 'leak' making it a race against time to do the dishes before all of the hot water runs out.

Cleaning the bathroom is widely regarded to be the least popular of household chores. When put off long enough only the nose-blind are able to ignore the nasal protests of a public health infringement. To ensure cleaning is carried out before it's too late, Gareth Trounce undertakes all of his cleaning bare-handed, safe in the knowledge that if he has indeed left it too long he will very likely be off work and spending a lot of time sitting down in there.

Cleaning the oven might not become a chore if it was simply given a wipe down after each use.

However, Benedict Ruffshod waits until he can no longer see through the glass door then exerts a great deal of elbow grease cleaning the oven over several sessions. However, his final session, shown here, looks to be his scouring pad's 'end of days'.

For some, washing the car is almost a pleasure, caring for their pride and joy every weekend.

For others, washing the car is the only viable excuse for getting away from the wife and kids if there's no shed to hide away in. So, with the soaping, rinsing, drying, waxing, polishing and admiring, this chore could be made just as laborious as it needs to be.

Tidying the shed sounds like it should only be an annual chore, if that. But somehow sheds, just like garages and draws, seem to get messy as soon as their door closes.

Spike Rushton is sorely tempted to just throw everything away. Instead he will place large items at the front to hide all the smaller stuff behind.

Lawns need cutting far too often. They are always more trouble to maintain than they should be.

Brenda Seldom has just finished the first cut of the year and after three hours of hard work has found her missing garden path. However, she is not well pleased that the condition of lawn is now little better than when she started mowing.

Cleaning the gutters is certainly an annual chore. Every spring all of the dead leaves and moss need removing before the wet season, which used to be known as summer, begins in earnest.

As Jennifer Flop exhaustedly tugs more detritus from her guttering she is most vexed by her ladder continually jumping for joy, away from the wall.

Dusting may actually be enjoyable to some people.

Molly Coddlynn spends hours each day dusting her many shelves of heir-loom ornaments using her late husband Alf's blower-brush. It is the only item of his prized photography equipment which she didn't put straight in the bin, with his favourite slippers, just as soon as the ambulance left with his body.

Defrosting the fridge-freezer is one of those chores which will almost sort itself out, as long as it is not done mid-winter with the central heating off.

Edna Dromedary knows that it is time to defrost when the ice-box stops the door closing. She found it something of a coincidence that this was also when green mould often sought squatter's rights.

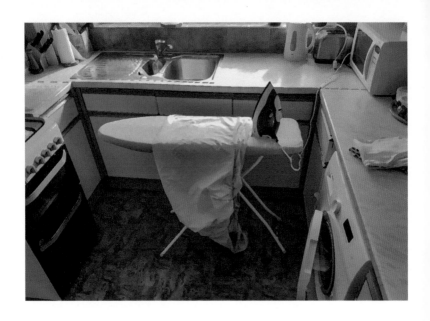

Ironing could be avoided by only wearing synthetics or simply not giving two hoots about appearances.

Graham Connelly finds that a ruined iron is a very good excuse not to continue with this chore. This tends to happen whenever he ends up with more creases than he started out with. He then recycles his irons in the council's 'Damaged irons bin'.

For those who do not want the responsibility of owning a pet, feeding the garden wildlife with waste food comes a close second.

Teri Macclesworth finds it a chore breaking up stale bread for the birds. She wonders why they can't do this for themselves. It's not like they have a job to go to.

Even when a car has been serviced it is advisable to check, oil depth, tyre pressure, washer liquid and other essentials before a journey.

Patricia Smedley plans to drive across to Iceland, so she is topping up the screen-wash, even though she only wants two pizzas and a tub of ice-cream.

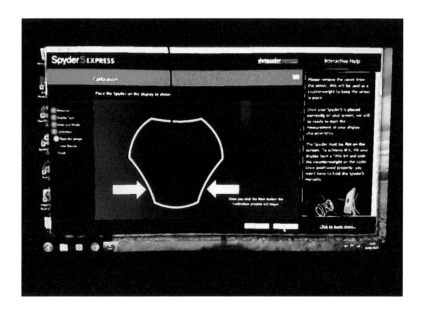

Regular computer maintenance can easily be as frustrating as looking after a needy child, with their constant requests for attention.

Another monitor calibration, defrag, or content back-up, and still it will drag its heels and look to further complicate activities wherever possible. You may well start asking yourself, Where's the love?

Not everyone has, or can afford, a coal fire these days. Denise Weatherspoon finds it quite a chore to battle past the bushes to her hidden stash of coal, especially on a cold, wet and windy night, to put half a dozen shovelfuls in her scuttle before locking the bunker down and returning to her fire before it goes out. At times she has found it easier and cheaper to simply burn the clothes and shoes which fast-fashion has cluttered her home with.

Ronald Green is a keen up-cycler. He would rather mend or alter old clothing than throw it away. However, he isn't perfect. If there is one thing that drives him to anger, more than getting the needle threaded then having the thread come straight back out once he touches the foot pedal, it's him, mis-stitching. So he reminds himself to focus with the mantra: 'You do do wrong Ron, you do do wrong.'

It might be a British standard to fit metres in inaccessible places, under stairs or at the back of cupboards but it certainly makes it a chore when the email arrives every month demanding another metre reading. After all, every six months should be adequate since the billing system should be able to estimate from previous years of readings what is being used, but *Oh no!* complains Shona Count.

Stephany Coaldraw has had it with duvet covers. Even when she buttons them closed for the wash they always manage to swallow all the other items.

Setting a bonfire raging in the back garden, Stephany hangs all of her clean duvet covers on the washing line to learn by example, popping the latest offender on the flames to smoulder mercilessly.

Retail therapy usually refers to shopping for clothes that are not needed, certainly not grocery shopping.

Melany Windscale-Hopkins, would like to shop at Waitrose, with having a double-barrelled name, but can only afford to patronise certain saver shops. Still, it takes her hours of traipsing up and down the aisles wondering what she might just keep down.

Perry Manopaws hated cutting the hedges more than once a year, so told his wife it was best done in the autumn to avoid killing their nesting birds.

He found it most reassuring that even when his arms grew dreadfully tired the trimmer still had the strength to cut through thick twigs just as easily as its power cord.

The idea of raised beds is to keep gardening tidier and to reduce the amount of bending down required. However, Colin Makepeace found these more than a chore to maintain. The fork kept getting stuck against the edging-stones and then, when he lost his balance one day, thanks to his size thirteen feet getting trapped in the channel between, he broke both ankles, the sound of which scared the birds out of the trees.

Kylie Corkindale had a problem with Fluffy, her cat, ignoring the mice that were getting into the house. She had even tried pointing them out. However, Fluffy would rather sit and moult. She tried humane traps first but the mice were too clever. So Kylie invested in a number of killer traps. That evening there came a promising squeal shortly followed by another. The cheese had proven irresistible, as curiosity caught the cat, twice.

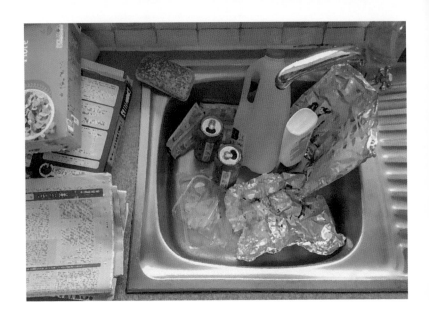

Since the fuel crisis and other criminal scams, Ingmar Rouche lived in fear of a fine or a jail sentence in her nineties. She had been told, in no uncertain terms, that all recycling must be washed thoroughly before being dried and then sorted. This took a great deal of soap and hot water and she often cried when her newspapers turned to Papier Mache. Whatever was the world coming to?

One idea for reducing the variety of garden chores is to fill in the garden pond and create a bog garden for plants that thrive in very wet soil.

However, on reflection one evening, Harry Hornby finally decided that fewer cats would be digging up his plants if only he had thought to remove the fish.

Vacuuming as a chore becomes so much worse on certain surfaces. Rugs appear to operate some sort of one-way system where the vacuum is strongly discouraged from travelling against the given direction. Matt Krauss also noted that some rugs behave like dust magnets. Their greed for dust knows no end as they actively draw the contents of the vacuum cleaner back out like a stomach pump.

Deirdre Fairway has complained to the council on numerous occasions. She doesn't have the room for all of their bins or the mental capacity to remember which collection days for which bins. There are four outside the back door and a further nine in her garden spoiling the view of her flower-beds. These bins are for plastic, glass, cans, foil, cardboard, landfill, garden waste, clothing, ash, batteries, junk mail, medical waste and pet hair.

It's one thing to wash windows at ground level but when it comes to first and second floor windows they are another storey.

Dave Pedimeister bought double glazing so that he could get a break from washing windows for a few months. As he stands procrastinating, his neighbour points out that he could just pay a window-cleaner.

Weeding is such a thankless chore. No sooner is a weed out than something is taking its place, looking to reclaim your property.

Underneath all these thistles, brambles and ivy is a drystone wall, and the breeze rustling through the nettles, where once had been a lawn, sounded to Mark Merriweather like 'Jussst leave usss.'

The local tip likes to charge for taking building materials even if you are not a contractor, so some people place a little of their DIY spoils with their landfill each week.

Unfortunately, Dennis Motley was never a patient man. He has loaded the bin with so many bricks that wheeling the bin out he has done his back in.

Every few years the paintwork in the house needs redoing. This is where the phrase 'Maybe next year' is not considered inappropriate.

At Selwyn Beagle's house however, the double glazing men have helped bring his need for painting forward by damaging the window sills in ways which were previously never considered possible.

Decluttering. Where did all these things come from? Horded away in cupboards and draws, once the attic had been filled. There are books, magazines, children's toys, clothes, and defunct technology like tapes, CDs plus a toastie and smoothie maker.

Charity shops are crying out for some of this stuff to go straight to landfill, as no one will take it for free.

Dry cleaning labels mean don't try machine washing and yet people still give it a go then wonder why they need a new washing machine after their 10Kg eider-down seals its demise mid-spin.

Sometimes no label is required because it's clearly a no-brainer. For Emma T. Cranium it'll be curtains.

Available on Amazon:

Titles in this series

The Cynic's View of Wilderness Walking
The Cynic's View of Enthusiastic Twitching
The Cynic's View of Watching Nature
The Cynic's View of Photographic Judging
The Cynic's View of Imaginary Friends
The Cynic's View of Laborious Chores

Other books by Kevin H. Hilton

Breakfast's in Bed
Imogen Powers - Possession
Imogen Powers - Afterlife
Imogen Powers - Singularity
Rhymes With
Rapid Prototypes for Free
Northern Darks
Dark Net
Admissions
Misadventure
The Newsagent
Project C-Spray
All in Bad Time
Night Porter

Printed in Great Britain
by Amazon